Sit

Sit

Stories by

Deborah Ellis

Groundwood Books
House of Anansi Press
Toronto   Berkeley

Groundwood Books / House of Anansi Press
groundwoodbooks.com

We acknowledge for their financial support of our publishing program the Canada
Council for the Arts, the Ontario Arts Council and the Government of Canada.

 Canada Council   Conseil des Arts
for the Arts   du Canada

 ONTARIO ARTS COUNCIL
CONSEIL DES ARTS DE L'ONTARIO
an Ontario government agency
un organisme du gouvernement de l'Ontario

With the participation of the Government of Canada
Avec la participation du gouvernement du Canada | Canadä

Library and Archives Canada Cataloguing in Publication

Ellis, Deborah, author
Sit / Deborah Ellis.
Short stories.

Issued in print and electronic formats.
ISBN 978-1-77306-086-6 (hardcover). — ISBN 978-1-77306-110-8 (softcover)
— ISBN 978-1-77306-087-3 (HTML). — ISBN 978-1-77306-088-0 (Kindle)

I. Title.

PS8559.L5494S58 2017   jC813'.54   C2017-900416-6
C2017-900417-4

Jacket illustration by Clare Owen
Jacket design by Michael Solomon

Printed and bound in Canada

 MIX
Paper from
responsible sources
FSC
www.fsc.org   FSC® C004071

 ANCIENT FOREST ™
FRIENDLY

To all who just need a moment of peace.

Contents

Contents

1

The Singing Chair

Jafar was sitting on a work bench in the furniture factory.

Not sitting, exactly. Perching, like a little bird on the edge of a trash can, ready to take flight at the first sign of danger from a cat or a truck.

Or from the boss storming through looking for slackers.

As he rested his bony little body, Jafar stared into a sunbeam. It was only a second-hand sunbeam, one that bounced off the window of the coffin shop across the lane, but Jafar looked forward to it every day. It meant his workday, which began in

Jakarta's pre-dawn gray, was heading toward the end.

The second-hand sunbeam pushed through the factory gloom. It made the men and boys glow like angels as they bent over their work. The dust particles danced and sparkled in the air.

I'm in a gold factory, Jafar thought.

In the haze, the rows and rows of chairs looked like thrones meant for gods and goddesses, not just kings and queens. No wonder the workers were not allowed to sit on them.

"Don't sit on the chairs!" Boss was always yelling at them. "The chairs are not for you and your filth."

Jafar had to agree with Boss about that. All the boys and men in the factory were filthy. Even Boss, although he was not nearly as dirty as the rest of them.

One of Jafar's jobs was to sweep. He swept the whole factory floor several times a day, but the dirt kept coming. Wood dust, wood shavings, grime from the sooty car and bus engines that blew in through the open wall that faced the street. The factory refused to stay clean while work was going on.

The dirt stuck to him, too. No matter how careful Jafar was with the glue and lacquer, drops always landed on his skin and clothes, and everything stuck to these drops. At the end of an especially busy day, when they rushed around to get their work done, sawing and sanding to fill orders, Jafar looked like some new kind of animal, with wood shavings for fur and soot-dust for skin. When he scratched his head with his glue-hands, the glue and wood dust made his hair stand up on the top of his head like many small ears.

"Quit daydreaming!" Boss yelled. He slapped the back of the boy's head as he moved through the factory.

Jafar jumped. He felt a little guilty because he *had* been daydreaming. He was working, though, and quickly. He could work with his hands and still daydream in his head.

Jafar was sanding chairs today, the final sanding before the chairs would be loaded on a truck and taken away. His chairs would go on a journey and he would be left behind.

Who would sit on his chairs? Would it be a happy person or an angry person? Would someone sit on one of his chairs and give up on life? Would his chair be a place where a child learned arithmetic or where an old man sat to eat a meal?

Would someone sit on one of his chairs to watch a sunbeam and keep watching as shadows grew and turned into night?

Jafar wanted to know, and he knew that he would never know.

These were not chairs that would be painted or polished. These were cheap chairs. They would be sold to people who still had to work hard and save long to buy them. The fancier chairs Jafar's factory made were beyond those people, and the real carpenters worked on those. Boys like him worked on the cheaper ones.

Jafar didn't care about not working on the fancy chairs. Work was work. Each day he worked brought him closer to paying off his family's debt, closer to being able to keep the money he earned, closer to having a life where his belly was always full and he could take the time to find work in a place where the boss would not hit him.

"We would make perfect murderers," said Sanu, who was a year older than Jafar but had only been at the factory for one year. Jafar had been there for three.

"What are you talking about?" Jafar asked.

Sanu held up his hands and wiggled his fingers.

"No fingerprints!" he said, laughing.

They could laugh now, but when Jafar first started sanding, his fingers got so sore and bloody!

"Get one more drop of blood on one of my chairs, you little cockroach, and I'll send you back to your family in a garbage sack!" Boss had yelled at him.

One of the older boys had slipped Jafar a blood-stained rag.

"My fingers have healed," he said. "You can have this now."

"How much do I pay you?" Jafar asked.

The older boy shrugged. "Someone gave it to me. Pass it on to someone else when you're done with it."

The blood stayed off the chairs, Jafar was not sent home as garbage, and his fingertips grew tough and strong.

"No fingerprints. That's a good one," Jafar said to Sanu. "You should go tell the others. We could all be murderers!"

He laughed again, but he really needed Sanu to go to another part of the factory and leave him alone for a moment.

There was something he had to do, and he could not have any witnesses.

Sanu looked pleased with himself but made no effort to move.

"I'll tell them later," he said. "If I go over there now and tell them, they'll think it came from you. They think all clever things come from you."

Jafar looked at the rows of completed chairs. There were only a few left for him to sand. Then the whole lot would be loaded into a truck and driven away.

He could not miss his chance today! There would be other chairs and other chances, but he was ready today! Another day, he might not have the nerve.

Jafar decided to use an old trick. He started sanding viciously, really putting his muscles into making the chair leg smooth like milk, going at the bumps and slivers with all the strength of his bird-thin arms.

"What are you doing?" Sanu whispered. "The fellas have just got the boss used to the slower pace. You want the old quotas back? You want to keep working until midnight again?"

"I just feel like finishing up," Jafar said, not slowing down one smidgen.

"Sweat by yourself, then," Sanu said. He picked up the chair he was sanding and moved away to sit and sand more slowly with the others.

Jafar kept up his speed for a few minutes more until he heard the voice and stomp of Boss returning to the factory floor. He slowed his pace then, but kept the boss in his peripheral vision. He kept watch on everyone.

No one must guess his secret.

No one must guess that he went to school.

Boss had not told him he couldn't go, but Jafar suspected he would if he knew about it. Boss said nasty things to workers who were smarter than he was. The other boys would make fun of him, too, if they knew. They would poke him and trip him and tell him he thought he was too good for them.

They gave him a hard enough time the day they caught him writing on a piece of scrap paper with a tiny stub of a pencil.

They grabbed his pencil and would not give it back. They tried to get his piece of paper, too, but he would not let them see what he was writing. He popped the paper in his mouth and chewed it and swallowed it. They did not get to see what he thought about the beggar on the corner, how her face looked like sunshine when she smiled. They did not get to know his private thoughts.

Anyway, he had written it clumsily. The words scrawled on the paper did not at all match the thoughts and feelings in his head.

His teacher at the school for working children read them poems. Poems told him feelings he didn't know he had. Poems made his heart dance and his mind fly above the smoke and stench and sweat of the city.

How do writers do it? Jafar wondered for the millionth time.

Today, he had a whisper of an answer.

Today, he had completed his first poem.

He had worked on it for days, trying to find the words, the words that would say exactly what he wanted to say.

Today, the poem was done.

Six words.

Six words that told the story of him.

Six words. Today, he had to grab the time and

the privacy to write down his six words and send them off into the world.

Maybe someone would discover them. Maybe someone would discover them years from now when the smooth yellow-wood chairs were gray with age and dust, the smoothness battered with dents and scratches.

Jafar kept watch for his chance.

He saw his moment.

He took a nail from his pocket. He lowered himself to the floor, tipped over the chair he was sanding and scratched his six words into the underside of the seat.

> *With this chair*
> *I am there.*

Boss would not like the poem on the chair. He would see it as damage. He would certainly hit Jafar if he found it, and make him pay for the damage with months and months of labor.

But Jafar needed his poem to leave his head. He needed to see it written down, and when he did, it was more beautiful than all the stars and all the flowers and all the kittens that ever were.

Quickly he pocketed the nail again and stood the chair up on its legs. He placed it in the row with the others.

Astonished at his boldness, adrenaline dashing through him, he finished sanding his last chair and put it with the others, too.

"What are you standing around for?" Boss yelled at him. "You think those chairs are going to load themselves? Move!"

Jafar carried chair after chair into the truck. The chair with his poem on it looked like all the others. But to Jafar's touch, it hummed and buzzed with life. *His* life.

The driver got into the truck and started the motor.

There was clean-up to do, sweeping and more sweeping. But Jafar leaned on his broom and watched.

He watched the truck with his chair and his poem move off down the street, passing the coffin shop the sunbeam had abandoned, merging with the motorbikes, taxis and people.

Somehow, amidst the honking horns, revving engines, hawking merchants and crying babies, Jafar heard something else. Something wonderful.

He heard his chair. It was singing.

> *With this chair*
> *I am there.*

It was the happiest day of his life.

2

The Time-out Chair

Macie is sitting in the time-out chair.

The time-out chair is an ugly pink plastic chair with a picture of a dinosaur on it. The dinosaur has a bow in its hair.

When Macie was two, she loved this chair. She could climb into it all by herself. Now that she is seven and knows that dinosaurs do not wear ribbons, the chair is an insult.

"If you don't like the chair, then don't do anything that makes you have to sit in it," Mommy says.

Mommy likes the chair. She points it out when people come to visit.

"Yes, this is our china cabinet," Mommy says to all the people who come over. "We got it just two years ago, ordered it special from the city. Ignore the little pink chair in the corner. That's Macie's time-out chair. She *lives* in that chair, don't you, Macie?"

Mommy laughs after she says that, and all the visitors laugh with her.

Then they say things like, "Eleanor, how in the world do you get her to sit there? I can't get my Bradley to do anything." And, "Can I borrow your chair, Macie? I could use a little time-out!"

The worst is like today, when the house is full of company and Mommy catches Macie with a bad attitude.

"I have to take time away from my guests to deal with you again," Mommy is saying, standing very tall beside the very short chair. Macie feels small beside her but she wants to feel smaller. The time-out chair is in a corner of the dining room. All the ladies are gathered around the table having cupcakes and coffee.

They can hear Macie being told off. They can see her sitting too-big in the too-small chair.

Macie is facing the corner but she knows they are staring at her.

"When I ask you to do something, I expect you to do it. Is that asking too much? If you had fetched the napkins from the pantry when I asked, we could have avoided all this. But you had to open your mouth and be all smart, telling me you'd do it in a minute."

You brought this on yourself, thinks Macie.

"You brought this on yourself," says Mommy. "When I tell you to do something, just do it. Life would be so much easier! She will *not* stop answering me back!" Mommy says to her guests. "She loves the sound of her own voice."

Mommy winds up the kitchen timer.

"I do two minutes for each year of her age," Mommy tells her company. "The experts say one minute but they don't know Macie! Fourteen minutes, young lady. Sit there and be quiet. None of your crying! No one here cares."

Macie is not crying, not one tear.

Mommy puts the timer down where Macie can see it and goes back to her chair at the table.

"More coffee, anyone? There's lots here and I can always make more."

The ladies pick up the chatter about the coffee. "I'll have a little more." And, "Where did you get these cupcakes? Are they from Betty's Bakery? I hope they are calorie-free!" Which makes them all laugh, although Macie can't understand why.

"I really shouldn't have one, but they look so pretty! Dare I? Do you think I should?"

Just eat the damn cupcake, Macie thinks. She happily rolls the swear word around in her head.

No one is talking about Macie, but everyone knows she is being punished and she knows that they know. When the buzzer goes off, she will have to get up off the stupid pink dinosaur chair and apologize to her mother in front of all the company. Her mother will lecture her again, then give her a cupcake and send her to the front porch to eat it. She can't be trusted not to drop crumbs on the floor if she eats it in the living room, and there is no room for her around the dining-room table.

When the ladies leave they will pass right by her on the porch and say things like, "Did you enjoy your cupcake?" And, "I'm coming by to borrow your special chair one day, Macie," which will make her feel worse than if they ignore her. If they talk to her, she'll have to talk to them in return, with a little smile plastered on her face. And she'd better be polite about it, or she'll be right back in the time-out chair!

"Macie? Are you being good?"

"She's being very good, Eleanor," says Mrs. Sardee from two doors down.

"She's probably sitting there scheming. What are you scheming about now?" Mommy asks Macie.

Macie doesn't answer her. Talking is *verboten* in the time-out chair. *Verboten* is German for forbidden. They are not German, but Mommy and Daddy always use the German word and laugh, and that is another joke that Macie doesn't get.

There is silence behind Macie. Then Mrs. Grenville, mommy to Cindy who babysits sometimes, says, "It's such a lovely day. Why don't we take our coffee outside?"

This is a popular idea. Macie hears all the ladies push back their chairs

"Macie, if you move from that spot before the buzzer goes, I will know it. When the buzzer goes off, bring the timer out to me," Mommy says. "She tries to get away with everything. Honestly, I'm in for it when she's a teenager!"

Macie hears the ladies leave the dining room and head out to the wide covered front porch. She hears them pull the comfy outdoor chairs out from the wall and arrange them in a semi-circle so they can see each other while they talk.

Macie looks at the kitchen timer. Ten minutes left.

She hates sitting still! Her legs and feet want to move, to run, to carry her far away from here to the park two blocks away where she is not yet allowed to go to by herself even though she knows all about looking both ways to cross the street.

She squirms in the tiny seat, her seven-year-old legs too long for her two-year-old chair. Her knees press against her tummy. She can't stretch out because that will make the chair move, and if the chair moves, it will make a noise. Mommy will hear and say she's being bad and give her more minutes in the chair.

The sounds of the women's voices drift in from the porch, mixing with the *tick-tick-tick* of the kitchen timer.

Nine minutes.

Eight minutes.

Mommy will hear the buzzer go off. She'll yell, "Bring it to me," and Macie will have to carry the buzzing timer out to the porch so Mommy can turn it off in front of the ladies, even though Macie is completely capable of turning it off herself.

Then Mommy will look at Macie and say, "Well, what do you have to say for yourself?"

Macie will have to say, "I'm sorry I talked back and I'm sorry I didn't get the napkins when you asked for them," even though she was reading and just wanted to get to the end of the page before she put her book down. Besides, Mommy says "In a minute" all the time when Macie asks her to do things.

"And?" Mommy will ask.

"And I won't do it again," Macie will have to say.

Mommy will tell her, "Well, if you think you can behave, you can join us."

Where will she sit? Macie knows how many ladies there are and how many chairs are on the porch. All the chairs are now filled with ladies.

Mommy won't let her sit on the porch floor or on the steps in her company dress.

Mommy also won't let Macie stay in the house by herself.

"Who knows what trouble you'll get in," she'll say. "Get out here where I can keep an eye on you."

Macie could sit on someone's lap, but she feels too big for that now and she doesn't like the feeling of being held in place by someone's arms. Plus, the ladies are her mother's friends. They aren't hers.

Most likely, Mommy will say, "Bring out another chair."

The dining-room chairs are heavy. Too heavy for Macie to move.

The only chair they have that is light enough for Macie to lift and carry is the chair she is sitting on now. The ugly pink plastic dinosaur time-out chair.

She'll be small, sitting low, low, down below the adult chairs.

The ladies will talk over her head about things she doesn't understand or care about. If she is quiet, someone will say, "Macie is such a good girl, sitting like a lady." Or, "Macie, you're so quiet. Cat got your tongue?"

If Macie says something, Mommy will say, "Macie, be quiet, the adults are talking."

Six minutes.

I'd like to have a house in the trees, Macie daydreams. Not a tree house in the yard. Mommy would still be able to watch her there from the kitchen window. That sort of house would come with, "Be careful going up that ladder!" And, "Are you behaving up there?" Whenever Macie was bad, Mommy would declare, "That's it, no tree house this week."

Macie's house would be far away, surrounded by trees. She would make friends with the squirrels and jays and all the other creatures. They would bring her berries and honey to eat, and on cold nights the deer would come into her house and keep her warm.

One minute.

Macie is shocked that the time has gone by so fast. Building her house in the trees has taken her right out of the time-out chair.

But soon the buzzer will sound. Mommy will call for her and Macie will have to sit with the ladies on the porch, feeling small and trapped. Her forest house will disappear.

The noise of the voices is all outside. Inside, the house is calm and quiet. Macie is alone with her thoughts. She is free. She would like to stay that way a little longer.

She has an idea.

Does she dare?

Macie looks toward the voices on the porch. Mommy can't see her. No one can see her.

She inches her hand out toward the kitchen timer.

She will pay for this later, she knows.

Mommy will find a reason to be mad at her about it, and for years after she'll say to her friends, "Let me tell you what my terrible, defiant daughter did." She'll tell it as if it was a big joke.

Everyone will laugh at me, Macie thinks.

Then she thinks, *Maybe I'll just tell them all to shut up.*

Macie takes hold of the ticking kitchen timer and turns the buzzer off before it can buzz. She puts it gently back in its place.

In her head, then, she floats up out of her punishment chair, heads deep into her forest house and gives herself a well-deserved time-out.

3

The Question Chair

Gretchen was sitting on a toilet.

She knew she shouldn't be. The whole place was a museum. Everyone knows you're not supposed to sit on things in museums.

But Gretchen needed to know — not that she ever could know, but she had to *try* to know — what it had been like. When the others in her class went outside to the train tracks, she slipped away and came back here.

And sat down.

Gretchen had never seen a toilet like this before, and she had seen some weird toilets in her travels with her family. She had seen a toilet in Japan that played music. At King Henry VIII's old palace in England, she saw a fancy box with fur on the seat, placed in the middle of the bedroom. Some unfortunate servant had to wipe the royal bottom.

This toilet was stranger than all of them.

It was not one toilet. It was many.

It was a long row of holes. People would sit facing both ways along it, down the length of the shed. The holes were staggered, like seats in a movie theater. People would sit back to back and shoulder to shoulder.

Gretchen sat over a hole in the middle of the long toilet and tried to imagine how it had been.

She tried to imagine the stench. She tried to imagine the tired, hurting, hungry people, shivering in their thin, lice-filled clothes. She tried to imagine the yelling of the guards — "Schnell! Schnell!" — giving the prisoners no peace even in this most basic and universal of human moments.

It was a latrine with no towels, no tiles, no paper, no door to close. No brushes, no combs, no makeup, no soap. No mirror, no hairdryer, no moisturizer, no gel.

Just a trough with holes.

If Gretchen had been one of those prisoners back then, she would have been one gray-striped person among many. Her hair would have been shaved off. She had already seen the pile of human hair in one of the large glass display cases. There was a display case of stolen shoes, too, and eye-glasses and suitcases.

If she had been a prisoner here, she would have been stripped of everything that was important to her.

She would be hungry, exhausted and beyond terrified.

"Would I still feel like myself?" she whispered. "Would the part of me that's me still be in me?"

Another thought entered her head.

I'm not Jewish. I wouldn't be here.

Instantly, she felt relief. She breathed a little bit easier.

Then she had another thought.

I'm German.

Gretchen heard the voices of another tour group approaching. She stood up before they got to the toilet shed where she was sitting. She went outside and joined the others in her class on the platform beside the train tracks that ended at the camp.

"Some people would go one way and be sent directly to the gas chambers," the tour guide said. "Others who looked like they were strong enough to work would go another direction and have a slower death through starvation, beatings and disease."

The tour guide spoke with feeling, even though he must have talked about these things many, many times. But none of it seemed as real to Gretchen as the toilets. The crimes he talked about seemed too horrible to have really happened, like the whole place was a theme park for a horror movie.

Maybe it was because the day was so sunny. The sky was blue and the grass was green, and all the photos Gretchen had seen of this place during the war were gray.

Maybe it was because she had all her classmates with her, the same kids she saw at school every day. And they looked the same as they always did — healthy and well fed and in clean, colorful clothes.

Maybe it was because she knew the whole thing was just a tour. There was an exit coming up. She could just walk through it and no one would shoot at her.

Gretchen's friend Kris poked her in the ribs and held out her phone. It was playing a video of a kitten batting at the long ears of a beagle. The tour guide was talking about Josef Mengele, the Angel of Death. Gretchen did not want to look at the kitten or laugh, but she also didn't want Kris to think she wasn't fun. She looked down at the screen and made her face grin.

Looking up again, she caught the tour guide watching them. He shook his head and led the group to the visitors' center and the exit.

"What did you think, Gretchen?" her history teacher asked. They were eating sandwiches in the parking lot before taking the tour bus back to Krakow.

Gretchen had just taken a big bite of her cheese and tomato on a roll. She shook her head, which could mean, "My mouth is full," or, "I don't know what to say."

"Where are we going for dinner?" one of her classmates asked. "Can we go back to that fondue place in the old city again?"

"I don't want to go there," Kris said. "It's too fancy and it takes too long. I just want to grab something quick and then go to that club attached to the hostel. They're having karaoke tonight. We can show these Poles how it's done!"

"We don't all have to do the same thing, do we?"

"It's our last night. Let's have fun!"

"Don't any of you have any reaction to what you saw here today?" their teacher asked.

"We learned all this in school," Kris said. "This year, last year, the year before that. You want us to feel guilty? We didn't do this." She waved her arms at the gray buildings and barbed wire behind them. "How many times do we need to apologize for what our ancestors did?"

"So, where *are* we eating tonight?" someone asked.

The teacher sighed. "Eat where you want," she said, and then she climbed onto the bus.

"Isn't she supposed to make sure we've got all our belongings or do a head count?" Kris asked. "How lazy can you get? And what are *you* moping about?"

"I'm not moping," said Gretchen. "Yeah, she's lazy."

Gretchen went along with Kris to the club. She pretended to have fun and cheered while Kris and others belted out songs, but she found the beat of the music annoying and wished she had stayed on her bunk in the hostel. She felt unsettled and could not figure out why.

The next morning they all boarded the plane back to Berlin. The field trip was over.

Gretchen walked into her parents' apartment on a pretty street not far from the train station. She hugged her mother and her father. She told them she'd had a good time and gave them the Krakow dragon salt and pepper shakers she'd bought at the airport gift shop. She unpacked her bags, then went into the bathroom and closed the door.

She brushed her teeth in front of the mirror. She looked at the lavender-scented soap in the soap dish, felt the soft, thick towel on the rack. She looked at the door, firmly shut against intruders, and felt a little sick.

Things got worse for her the next day.

She saw reminders of the war everywhere. Things she had seen every day for her whole life but had never taken any notice of now seemed to jump out at her.

Things like a stop on the rail line called Spandau, where the prison used to be that held the head Nazis after their trial in Nuremberg.

Things like the Reichstag, the German parliament building where Hitler had reigned.

Things like the highway signs that read *Wannsee, 10 km.*

Wannsee was where Reinhard Heydrich, Adolf Eichmann and others planned the extermination of the Jewish people.

She saw a sign for Sachsenhausen, a concentration camp a few kilometers away.

How close it was to the city! Didn't people wonder what was going on there during the war? With all the people who worked there — building the place, guarding the place — surely someone must have talked. People must have known. Had anyone tried to stop it?

"We've always lived in Berlin, haven't we?" she asked her parents at dinner. It was Italian night. Her father had made his specialty, veal scaloppine. "I mean, I know *we* have, but your parents and grandparents were also all Berliners, weren't they?"

"Our great-grandparents, too, I think," said her father. "My great-grandfather was a cloth merchant. Imported cloth from France and Italy. Did very well, I'm told."

"So …" Gretchen found herself nervous to ask this next question, but she swallowed her nerves. "What did your grandparents do in the war?"

Her parents dropped their forks at the same time, as if they had rehearsed it.

Her mother was the first to pick hers up again and resume eating.

"You went to Auschwitz and came back with questions about the war," she said. "If you had gone to Switzerland you would have come back asking about chocolate and cheese."

That didn't make any sense to Gretchen. "Well, yeah."

"Young people are so self-righteous," her mother said. "You are so eager to question things, to say that you would have done things better and the people before you were all stupid and morally bankrupt."

"I didn't say that."

"The war was a terrible time for everyone. What would you know about terrible times? You visit one little concentration camp and think you have a right to question your great-grandparents. Be grateful you do not have to face what they faced."

That was all Gretchen's mother would say. Her father said nothing at all.

Gretchen skipped school the next day. She went to the chalet at Wannsee where the extermination had been planned. It was now a museum. She spent the day looking at the photos, reading the history and sitting by the lake, trying to make sense of it all. She did not tell her parents. She did not tell anyone.

Gretchen started to read about Germany before the war and about the rise of hatred. She searched her school library and spent her pocket money in bookstores in the Alexanderplatz shopping district. She read *Hitler's Willing Executioners* and memoirs of concentration camp survivors.

Strange things began to happen to her vision.

Walking down the street, she saw tall, healthy German men standing in a group talking. They all wore the uniform of the Nazi SS.

Gretchen wanted to scream out at them, but when she looked again, they were just wearing rugby clothes, grass-stained from a pickup game in the park.

Her algebra teacher pointed at an equation on the board, but all Gretchen saw was the Nazi swastika.

She watched the boys at her school, especially the blond ones with blue eyes, the ones eager to participate, eager to build and do and go, and she saw them all in the uniforms of the Hitler Youth.

In another era, not so long ago, they would have been.

"You're no fun anymore," Kris told her. "Brighten up, will you?"

Gretchen did not feel like brightening up. She moved through her school days alone.

The worst night of all was back at her family's supper table.

Gretchen's father — her tall, fit, capable father — was somehow transformed before her eyes into an officer of the Gestapo.

Would that have been his choice? He was a cultured, educated man. Would he have been different seventy years ago? Would he have worked at Sachsenhausen, as a guard, perhaps, or as an administrator, putting numbers and names on pieces of paper and then filing them away neatly as the bodies piled up?

Gretchen looked away from him and at her mother, a smart, strong, ambitious woman. Today she was a lawyer at a big corporation. Back then? What would a woman like her mother have done? Women joined the Nazi party just like men did.

Women went to the rallies. Women hit prisoners and made fun of Jews and did not object when families disappeared in the middle of the night. Her mother loved success. How would she have defined success during the Nazi times? Who would her mother have chosen to be?

"May I be excused?" Gretchen asked, looking down at her half-eaten meal. "I have a lot of homework."

"Rinse your dishes," her mother said, the same thing she said after every meal. Gretchen rinsed her plate, put it in the dishwasher and went to her room.

She could not look at her parents anymore.

I have to move out, she thought, sitting on her bed. *Where will I go?* She suddenly felt so lonely.

She realized with great grief that there was no part of her that thought her parents would have been on the right side of things. She *knew* they would not have lifted a finger to help a Jewish family because they didn't lift a finger now to help the homeless or the environment or even stray cats. If they did not do that sort of thing now, why would they have done it if they had been alive seventy years ago?

Heartbroken, Gretchen got ready for bed.

She went into the bathroom to brush her teeth.

She looked in the mirror.

Instead of her present-day self in her sky-and-cloud pajamas and red headband, she saw her 1940s self. Her blonde hair was in two tight braids at the side of her head. She wore the uniform of the Bund, the girl version of the Hitler Youth. Her eyes were steel and her face was hard.

On a band around one arm was a swastika.

Gretchen realized then the real question she had been avoiding. The question of her life. It was not who would her parents have been.

It was who would *she* have been?

At this moment, she was not sure.

Did *she* help anyone? Did she stand for anything? What did she believe? Did she decide things for herself or did she allow her friends to decide for her?

If she were alive when the Nazis were in power, whose side would she be on?

Whose side was she on today?

I want to know, she thought. *I have to know.*

Maybe it was her imagination, but with that resolve, her reflection seemed to change. There was a softening in the glare of her eyes, a relaxing in the meanness of her jaw. The improvements were slight, but they were there. They were!

Maybe there was a chance for her.

Questions, she thought. *I'll keep asking questions.*

Maybe, someday, she would have answers.

4

The Knowing Chair

Barry was sitting on a red metal chair that was attached to a metal table in the food court of the mall.

He was waiting for his parents to decide what they would all eat. He settled in for a long debate.

"I'm not running all over the place to get forty different meals," his father always said, even though there were only four of them in Barry's family. "Pick one."

They usually settled on the pizza place. Not the one where you could get meatballs on the pizza but the other one, where Mom could get a salad.

It would take them a long time to get around to that, though.

"We're going to let you both choose your own suppers tonight," his father said.

"Really?" asked Sue, Barry's seven-year-old sister. "Anything? Like, three desserts?"

"Don't be foolish," their mother snapped, then softened her tone. "Suey, go with Daddy. Barry, here's some money. Go get your own. I'll stay here and hold the table."

"Really?" Barry knew he sounded like a little kid, but he couldn't help it as he stared down at the bills his mother placed in the palm of his hand.

"It's time you were more self-sufficient," she said. "You're too old to have everything done for you all the time. Go on. We want to make that movie."

Supper out *and* a movie. On a school night! Aliens had clearly taken over Barry's parents. He pocketed the money and went on a tour around the food court.

He would *not* get pizza, or a burger, or a hot dog, or a sub. Those were safe things, boring things, foods old people or a little kid might choose.

No, he would exercise his freedom of choice on wild things, exotic things. Things that would show his family he was not afraid of adventure. His meal would become a story.

"You should have seen what Barry chose," he could imagine his mother saying on the phone to one of her nosy friends. "I had no idea he was such a brave eater."

Barry filled up his tray with a fish taco, Japanese noodles with shiitake mushrooms, and four little Chinese moon cakes, one for each person in his family to try.

He carried it all back to the table where the others were already eating.

And what had Sue chosen? Cheese pizza! Barry sat tall with his three extra years of adventurous spirit keeping his head high. The chili sauce on the fish taco was a bit too strong and the mushrooms in the noodles tasted like erasers, but he did not let on.

Sue was chattering, as usual, like a cage full of monkeys. Barry let her have all their parents' attention. That left him free to indulge in his favorite hobby — watching people.

Barry suspected it was wrong, but he often imagined that every person on the planet was some kind of zoo animal, there for him to watch and think about.

At the next table an old guy in a brown suit was eating something in a pita. He was all by himself at the table, and he read while he ate, some sort of work report. Barry could see charts on the old guy's paper. A dollop of pita sauce dropped on one of the charts. Barry watched the man frantically dab at it with his napkin.

That won't help, Barry thought. He'd dropped enough food on enough homework to know it always left a mark.

At another table sat another family. It looked just like his family only with an extra kid. The mom was nagging at the middle kid — a boy — while the dad stared down at his phone. The mom's face was scrunched tight and her finger was pointed in her son's face. One of the children was a girl about Barry's age. She caught him watching her and she looked away, embarrassed.

Barry's eyes shifted to a gray-haired woman sitting across from a little girl at one of the tables for two. The little girl was Sue's size. The old woman leaned in toward her with a smile on her face that overflowed to her eyes. She was hanging onto the little girl's every word, and the two of them looked as happy as sea otters.

The table down from those two was a different story.

The man and woman were both looking at their phones, ignoring their little boy who was having trouble lifting his massive burger with his tiny hands. Every few moments one of the adults would snarl something at the other. Barry couldn't hear exactly what they said because of the noise in the food court, but he recognized the short, sharp tones and the rolling eyes and the dismissive shakes of their heads.

It's always the same, Barry thought. *People argue in public places and think no one knows that they're fighting.*

He spotted the telltale signs of posture and face, the sharpness of shoulders and stiffness of chins that showed anger and hatred.

Julius Caesar and Cleopatra probably looked the same when they fought, Barry thought. He wanted to list off other famous fighting couples in history but realized he didn't know any.

Research for tomorrow, he promised himself.

"There's a van!" squealed Sue.

"Inside voice," said Mom.

"A van! A camper van!" Sue said only slightly less loudly.

"We're in a mall, Suet," Barry said. "There's no van in a mall."

"Uh-huh!" insisted Sue, kicking Barry under the table for calling her Suet. She pointed toward the end of the food court.

She was right. Next to the elevators, a light blue VW camper van was set up like a food truck.

"Oh," said Dad. "I didn't see that before."

"Stop pointing, Suey, and eat," said Mom.

"Is that why you brought us here on a school night?" Sue asked. "Are we going on the trip?"

The trip. The trip Barry had been hearing about all his life.

"Wouldn't it be great to take you kids out of school for a year and just travel?" his parents had said many times, dreaming over their collection of maps. "We could live in an old VW van and you can learn all about the country. Not from a geography book but from seeing it and living in it."

Every summer, as they got closer to the opening of the school year, Barry hoped that this would be the year. *This* would be the September they hit the road instead of the schoolyard. The Trip would bring Barry so much freedom! His parents would be so busy keeping track of Sue that he would be able to slip away from time to time to explore new places and watch the new people in them.

His parents would send him on errands to get milk when they got to a new town, or they'd ask him to sit with the laundry in the laundromat, or they'd say things like, "Go find the manager of this camp ground and ask if we can stay an extra week because Sue's been asked to a birthday party."

He would have so many chances to be on his own, to wander without an adult to police him, to think his own thoughts without a parent intruding, to see different people and think about what they were doing without his mother saying, "I've told you before it's rude to stare," and without his father saying to his mother, "Can't you get him to *do* something?"

Was Sue right? Was this why they were out on the town on a school night?

"Can we go see all the big things?" Sue asked, as she always did whenever The Trip came up. "Can we go stand right up beside the giant nickel in Sudbury? Can we take a picture of me by the big nickel holding up a little nickel? Can we go to Dunnville and see the giant catfish? And then the giant Easter egg? Can we go to the giant apple and walk around inside it? And can you take a picture of me eating a regular-sized apple outside the giant apple?"

Sue had no idea of what was close to what, but she sure did know her giant attractions. She was so excited!

"We'll do our school lessons on the computer and Barry will help me with my arithmetic, won't you, Barry? Remember? You promised!"

"Sure, I'll help you," said Barry. "Are we really going?" The Trip had been talked about so often and in such detail — down to packing lists — but had never materialized.

Barry was a little nervous about getting too excited, because he was afraid of being disappointed again.

Sue would not shut up about the giant statues.

"Maybe we could make them come alive with magic and the giant moose will follow us down the highway. There's a giant goose, too. The goose will fly and the moose will walk and we'll be a parade of giant creatures that are really, really big but they will be really gentle, too."

Their parents let Sue prattle. Their mom kept spearing lettuce with her plastic fork, and their father separated the pizza slices in the box.

They wouldn't let her go on about it if it wasn't going to happen, would they? Barry thought.

Trying to contain his own excitement, he looked around the food court, checking in on the people he had watched earlier.

The man in the suit was stuffing papers in his briefcase. He had not noticed the blob of pita sauce on his necktie.

The little girl and the old lady were giggling. They had soaked their paper napkins in the woman's cup of water and were molding them into creatures as if the wet paper was modeling clay.

The arguing couple were still snarling. Their little boy had still not managed to take a bite of his burger. He looked unhappy and like he was afraid to really try.

"Oh, come on," Barry said. He got up from his red chair, went to the fighters' table and knelt down beside their little boy.

"Hey, buddy, let me help," Barry said to the boy quietly. He took the tomato and lettuce off the burger, because nobody wanted those. Then he used a plastic knife to cut the burger into four pieces. The little guy easily picked one up and started eating.

"What are you doing?" the dad asked Barry. The mom simply told Barry to take off, only she didn't say "take."

Barry smiled at the little boy and headed back to his own table.

He caught a glimpse of another arguing couple in one of the mirrors hanging all over the food court.

This couple had a little girl with them, around seven years old. They were watching the girl talk, but their faces said they were not listening to her. Their bodies were tense with sharp shoulders and stiff chins. They had themselves pulled far away from each other.

The woman looked at the man with disgust and the man looked back at the woman like he hated her.

Always the same, Barry thought.

Barry realized then that he was looking at his own parents.

He realized something else, too.

They had not brought him and Sue to the mall on a school night to tell them they were all going on a trip.

The supper and the movie were not treats. They were bribes.

They were *We are doing these nice things for you so you can't feel bad at what we are about to tell you and you won't dare make a scene in public because you both know we won't stand for that.*

The fish taco and the Japanese noodles went round and round in the boxing ring of Barry's stomach.

He sat down in his red metal chair. He looked full at his parents and they looked full at him.

They know that I know, he thought. *Good. Just try to lie to me. Just try.*

Barry took hold of his little sister's hand. She yanked it away.

Their mother said. "We've got something to tell you."

Barry kept his eyes on his parents through the whole unraveling, while Sue cried and his father cried and his mother said that she knew they should have told them at home. No one touched the moon cakes Barry had bought for them to try.

Barry did not cry and he did not speak. He glanced away from his parents' faces only once, to the girl his age at the table with the family sort of like his.

The girl was now watching him like he was an animal in a zoo. When she saw him look at her she did not look away. She grimaced and pointed her head toward her own idiot parents.

I'll get my own van, Barry thought. *I'll take Sue and we'll go see the giant nickel and we won't invite* them *to come with us.*

He tried to hold his sister's hand again.

She would not let him.

He kept on trying.

5

The Plain Chair

Jed was sitting on the schoolhouse fence. It was a plain wood fence, comfortable for sitting.

Jed had sat there many times after school, taking a moment to be with his friends before heading home to do afternoon chores. He had sat there at recess, eating apples and watching the younger ones play blind man's bluff. And when he was really small, he had sat there propped up by his mama's arm as he watched the bigger kids fly like birds out the schoolhouse door as soon as the bell rang.

Jed had never sat on the fence this early before. This was early, so early it was practically still yesterday. The stars were still out and the air was crisp with night chill.

It was even before morning chore time, before the cows were ready for milking, the eggs were ready for gathering and before the pigs were ready for their breakfast.

He would not do his morning chores today.

"You don't have to go," his mother had said again in their kitchen that morning. She made him eat a bowl of the porridge that had been cooking on the back of the woodstove all night. "There will be plenty of others there. I can't go. I know I can't."

"I have to go," Jed told her. "I want to."

But want was not the right word. There was nothing about this that he wanted.

Mama understood anyway, wrong word or not.

"Don't worry about your chores," she said. "I'll do them for you."

"You will?" he asked. "I mean, won't they be too hard for you?"

Mama gave him a playful swat on the head and reminded him that she had done his chores and plenty more back when he was too young to have enough sense to know which end of a cow to milk.

They smiled at each other. Just a wisp of a smile, but it was a smile all the same. It warmed Jed even as he wondered if it was right that they should smile so soon after The Day. Maybe it would never be right for them to smile.

Jed's father had been killed years ago when a drunk driver crashed into his horse and buggy. Jed was very small at the time, and he could no longer remember how long it took for his mother to laugh again after that.

Sitting on the fence now, Jed looked at his school through the dim light of the half moon and stars.

The school wasn't anything special. It was not like those fancy schools the English children went to in town, with inside bathrooms and many classrooms filled with shelves of books and rows of computers. Jed had never been in one of those schools, but Ezra Brubacher had gone for special help with his reading when he was smaller, and he told Jed all about it.

"They have baseball and movies and assemblies and library visits and art on the walls and all sorts of fancy things," Ezra told him. "If it's your birthday you get jelly beans. If you are Student of the Day you get to choose a bookmark from a box in the office."

Jed told Ezra it all sounded very exciting, but in his head he thought their plain way was better. All the classes in one room together, without all the noise and fancy stuff.

The sound of a horse's hooves broke into Jed's thoughts. He looked over his shoulder and saw Emmanuel's wagon coming down the lane. He got off the fence to help with the horse, looping the reins around a post. He and Emmanuel were soon joined by the Sauder boys (who everyone still called boys even though they were all past forty), by the Brubachers, the Martins and others. All the men from the community were there, except for the fathers. No one expected or even invited the fathers to be there.

The men unloaded their tools and walked through the gate into the schoolyard.

There were no community women. Usually at a gathering like this the women would show up in a few hours' time loaded with coffee cake, hard-boiled eggs and thick slices of cold ham.

Today, though, the women would be sitting with the hurt families, taking them food and comfort.

There were probably women heading to Jed's mother's house right now.

The sudden noise of car engines and the glare of headlights made everyone stop and turn.

"Is that the press?" Elijah Sauder asked. "Did they find out we were doing this and come to make a story out of it?"

"Maybe it's more of those gawkers, come for souvenirs," said Elijah's brother Ebenezer.

"Just wait," Abe Martin said calmly.

A line of vehicles and lights approached. Jed saw that they were pickup trucks filled with men and women from town. The mayor was with them. Usually the mayor was in a suit and tie. This morning, he was dressed for work in jeans and a sweater. All the townspeople wore work clothes.

"We are here to help," said the mayor.

Everybody shook hands. Then they all went to work. The townspeople left their truck headlights on, pointed at the school, to make it easier for everyone to see what they were doing.

"Jed, you stay with me," said Emmanuel. Emmanuel was in his mid-twenties and fairly new to the community. He had come from Wallenstein to marry Anna Freiberger and he taught Jed carpentry on Saturdays. "We'll work outside."

"I need to go in," Jed said.

"Are you sure?"

"I need to see," said Jed.

Emmanuel nodded. "We'll go together."

The men parted for Jed. Jed opened the schoolhouse door.

This is where that man came in on The Day, Jed thought. *He walked right in through this door. He saw the chalkboard just like I am seeing it now.*

The inside of the school looked like a scene from a dream. The headlights shining in from outside cast shadows where they had never been before.

It all looked strange, but Jed could still see the rows of plain desks. The big desks at the back were for the older students. The little desks at the front were for the young ones. Jed saw the woodstove and the alphabet cards on the wall.

Below the chalkboard, Jed could see the dark stains on the plank floor.

The teacher, Miss Steinman, had been teaching the fourth-grade class about the parts of a flower. The children were holding up the wildflowers they had picked at recess and were looking closely at the petals. Jed was at his desk, mid-way in the rows with his age group, closer to the back than the front. He was watching the flower lesson because it was more interesting than the geography book he was supposed to be reading.

The man walked into the school slowly, Jed remembered, but seemed to get to the front of the room before anyone really realized he was there.

"You — get up here," the man said. He pointed a gun at a boy in the front row, one of the second graders, and waved the gun toward the chalkboard.

The boy, little Daniel, who never seemed to grow into his older brother's hand-me-downs, went to the board. He picked up a piece of chalk. That's what children did when they went to the front of the schoolroom.

"Can I help you?" Miss Steinman asked.

Then, seeing the gun, she spread her arms out like a mother hen spreading her wings over her chicks.

"Please go," she said.

The man ignored her. He pointed to students at random, ordering them to the chalkboard.

Did it happen quickly or did it happen slowly? Was he shouting?

Jed didn't think so. He would have remembered that. People did not usually shout in the community. He would have remembered shouting.

Jed took steps toward the chalkboard, toward the spot where it all happened.

Jed's sister, Melinda, in the third grade, was one of the ones called up to the board. He could never imagine what the man would do. He had no way to imagine it.

Maybe, if I had known, I could have said something to change his mind, or done something to stop him, he thought. He took some more steps toward the front.

"Jed."

He felt a gentle hand on his shoulder.

"Jed, that's far enough," said Emmanuel. "There is no purpose in going closer. Let's put our grief to work."

Jed nodded. Work was why he was there.

He and Emmanuel carried out desks while others dismantled the woodstove. Already the windows were being taken out carefully to be reused in the new school. He heard the sound of shingles being pried off one at a time, framing being taken apart and lumber being stacked.

They all worked hard. Those with skills and strength did the heavy parts that required know-how. Those with less experience loaded wood and shingles into trucks and wagons. The floorboards were taken up, and even the fence Jed had been sitting on was dismantled.

The townspeople, who seemed to be constantly talking whenever Jed was among them in town, worked in silence like the rest of them, speaking only about the work, only in quiet tones.

Jed thought he might cry while he worked, but he didn't. He didn't think very much, either. He just worked.

I'm just doing chores, the same as every other day, he told himself. *Nothing different about this day.*

The sky went from black with stars to gray with a hint of mist. By the time the sun peeked up at the edge of the Brubacher farm, the school was down. All the parts were in trucks, much of it already taken to the new schoolyard, a corner of the Sauder farm two lanes down.

The rakes and shovels were brought out next. The ground where the school had been was smoothed over. Shrubs and clumps of wildflowers from people's yards and fields were put into the ground. Jed planted a maple sapling close to where he thought the chalkboard had been. There was no marker put on it, but he would remember.

The sun came fully up. Everyone shook hands. The trucks were loaded up with townspeople and the wagons with plain people.

"Hop on," Emmanuel said to Jed. "I'll give you a ride back."

"No," said Jed. "I walked here this morning. I'll walk home, too."

Emmanuel shook Jed's hand as if Jed was grown.

"Don't make your mother wait too long for you," he said. Jed promised he wouldn't.

He watched everyone drive away.

The last of the pickups and wagons had just disappeared from Jed's view when a new convoy of cars and trucks came driving up from another direction. The out-of-town media people got out and walked around in city clothes and shiny shoes.

"Where did the school go?" Jed heard them say from where he stood on the other side of the road. "This is the place, right? Did they move it? We were just here yesterday. Did they up and move a whole school?"

"I don't get these people," Jed heard someone else say. "Don't they want to remember? They don't even seem angry."

Jed turned his back on them and headed home.

Women from the community would be there. They would have a good breakfast ready for him, and would have helped his mother with all the chores.

Today, he could just be with his mother.

Tomorrow, he would add his sister's chores to his own.

He could shoulder both. That was something he could do.

6

The Day-off Chair

Bea was sitting on a wooden bench, pretending to read a book.

It was a daring place to sit. The bench was on the sidewalk right downtown.

Behind her was Oak Street. Not the main street in her town but pretty close to it. Her bench faced a little strip of shops — the Curly Clip where the old ladies went to get their hair done, the Green Dream yoga studio, a real-estate office with a window full of pictures of houses for sale, and a print shop that did wedding invitations.

The print-shop place had a fake wedding cake on display. From where Bea sat, she could see a thick layer of dust on the fake icing.

Farther down the street was a lawyers' office in one of the town's red brick historical buildings. A low hedge surrounded the yard. There was a big rock in that yard, perfect for little kids to climb on. To stop them, the lawyers hired someone to plant flowers around the rock. No parent would let their kids walk through a flowerbed, not even to let them have the joy of climbing up on a great big boulder.

Oak Street was not the busiest street in town, but lots of people still walked down it, and they all looked at Bea sitting by herself on a bench in the middle of a school day.

Bea didn't worry about the old ladies. She had sat on this bench before on her days off and the old ladies left her alone. Either they were afraid to confront her because kids scared them, or they remembered being young themselves at a time when a child could be alone on the street or in a shop or in a park without anyone thinking they were up to no good or about to be abducted.

The old ladies didn't care that she was sitting there. When Bea's grandmother was a girl, she used to go to the grocery store and the swimming pool and playground all by herself, returning home only when she got hungry or the streetlights went on.

The dangerous ones were the yoga ladies, with their mats rolled up under their arms and their noses in the air, looking all "If I can take time out of *my* busy day to be enlightened, there's no excuse for you!"

Bea wasn't being rude thinking that. She actually heard one lady say it to her teenaged daughter who was rounder than her mom and looked like she'd rather be going to the dentist than into a yoga studio with her mother.

The yoga ladies were busybodies. Bea had only been sitting on the bench for half an hour, and already three of the mat-toters had come up to her, nosiness dripping off their faces.

"Are you lost, honey?" one asked.

"Is everything okay?" asked another.

The third woman came right out with it. "Shouldn't you be in school?"

"I am ten years old and have lived in this town my whole stupid life, so, no, I am not lost. Everything will be okay as soon as you get away from me. And, yes, I should be in school but I'm taking the day off because I'm sick of people BUGGING ME!"

Bea said none of those things, of course.

Instead, she looked up from her book, smiled sweetly and said, "I'm just waiting for my mother. She's at the dentist. I've been already. My appointment was before hers. She told me to wait for her here since it's such a nice day. As soon as she's done she's going to drive me back to school."

That satisfied them. They went into yoga like the Queens of Neighborhood Watch. By the time their stretch class was finished, Bea would have moved to a different bench and they would have forgotten all about her.

The yoga ladies did not know Bea, and they did not know her mother.

Bea's mother did not like yoga. She liked drinking. She called it her "sport."

"I don't need to carry a rolled-up bed or wear a step-counter for my sport," she'd brag, cracking open the seal on a new bottle of gin.

"Maybe you should wear a drink-counter," Bea's father said.

They used to argue *while* drinking, but Bea's dad went to AA and now they argued *about* drinking.

Mom had dropped Bea off at school that morning as usual. It was a silent ride because Mom had a hangover, but it wasn't a quiet ride because Mom could get angry at anything at any moment. Mom's silent anger was very loud. She could drive and hit at the same time.

Bea got out of the car at school. She watched her mom drive away. She watched the kids run around the schoolyard. She saw the teachers through the classroom windows, busy setting out papers and hanging up artwork, getting ready for the day.

Bea could not move. She could not leave the sidewalk and head into the playground.

She wasn't afraid of being bullied. The teachers kept their eyes open at her school, so bullying wasn't really a problem. There were kids Bea liked and who liked her. Her teacher sometimes bugged her about paying attention, but that was nothing Bea couldn't handle.

There was no good reason she could not go to school.

"I just need a day off," she said.

Bea pointed her feet, walked and walked and finally sat down on the Oak Street bench.

It felt good to just sit. It felt good to be left alone with her thoughts, and to not think at all if she didn't feel like it.

Sit. She just wanted to sit.

She closed her eyes to shut out the world.

"Mom!"

Bea opened her eyes and looked for the owner of the voice.

"Mom!"

Bea saw a small boy, four or five years old. He was down in the lawyers' yard looking past Bea and up toward the main street.

Bea looked to where he was looking. A woman at the street corner was talking to an older woman who was waiting to cross the street to go in a different direction.

"Mom!"

The mom-woman looked down the street and gave her son a little wave, then continued her conversation.

Bea watched the boy jump up and down with excitement. She looked back at the mom and saw the traffic light turn green. The older woman said her goodbyes and started to cross the street. Bea turned back to the little boy just in time to see him duck behind the rock in the lawyers' yard.

He's going to jump out at her, Bea thought. *He's going to pop up and surprise her.*

The mom, walking now with purpose, got closer and closer.

"She's going to be shocked," Bea said out loud. "She'll jump back and she'll be embarrassed and she'll yell at him. She'll get mad at him for getting his clothes dirty and walking on the plants. Maybe she'll even hit him for scaring her!"

Bea could feel the sting of the slap on her own cheek.

The mom got closer to the rock.

Bea stood up. She could run fast. If the mom raised her hand to hit the boy, Bea would take off down the street, slam into the woman and knock her to the ground.

Bea imagined the little boy down behind the rock, peeking around it through the branches in the hedge, watching his mom get closer and closer, his muscles tight, giggling to himself, his legs getting ready to spring into action, until —

"Surprise," he shouted.

"Don't hit him!" Bea called out.

The mom jumped high and threw her arms up at the sight of her little boy. She opened her mouth — and laughed!

"You got me!" the mom said. "That was a good one!"

She put her arm around his shoulders. Bea heard the two of them laughing as they walked away together down the street.

Bea was shaking. She wiped tears off her face with the back of her hand.

"Sometimes things turn out all right," a voice said beside her. One of the old Curly Clip ladies had been watching the mother and boy, too. The lady put her old hand briefly on Bea's arm, then toddled off with her new hairdo.

Bea didn't want to sit anymore.

Her feet started walking again.

They took her back to her school and into her classroom.

Her teacher took one look at Bea's face and did not say a single word to her about being late.

7

The Glowing Chair

Miyuki was sitting on a tatami mat in the evacuation center.

The center was usually a high-school gymnasium. Now it was full of people who had run from their homes.

Miyuki's father stood over her.

"You cannot go back," he said. "How many times do I have to say this? You cannot risk yourself for a foolish donkey!"

"But she's Mother's donkey!"

"It's a foolish donkey. Your mother was a foolish woman, and you are a foolish girl."

Miyuki's father had been a teacher in the before-tsunami world. His school had been broken by the earthquake.

Miyuki didn't know what he was now, but he still lectured like a teacher.

"You cannot go into the danger zone," the lecture continued. "You will come out glowing with radiation. All your hair will fall out and you will get sick. At twelve years old, you should be able to understand that."

I understand it, Miyuki thought while she played with the buckles on her school bag in her lap. *I just don't like it.*

"The government has made these rules for us, and we will obey them. We do not break rules in this family."

"Mother broke rules," Miyuki said before she could stop herself. "She broke your rules."

His rules said that her mother could not study to be a veterinary technician. His rules said that she should stay at home and look after things there.

"Your mother agreed to those rules, and then she broke them," her father said. "Look where it got her."

Miyuki did not think that her mother going to

work was what caused the giant wave to swallow up the veterinary clinic and other shops and homes, but she did not say so.

Father loomed large over her, like a shadow in a bad dream. She did not look up at his face, but stared at the crease in his trousers. After three days at the evacuation center, the crease was less sharp, and the cuffs had picked up dust and bits of rice crackers.

"The donkey will be fine until we get back home," he said.

"How can you say Hisa will be fine if it's not safe for me to go back and get her?" Miyuki asked, unable to keep the anger out of her voice.

"Hisa? Who's Hisa?"

Miyuki clenched her fists to keep from screaming. "You know the donkey's name."

It was a game her father played with her. When she got angry, he got light. It always felt like he was making fun of her.

"I named you Miyuki so you would be silent, like a snowfall. I should have named you Nariko, because you are always noisy, like thunder. All I have to say to you is that your constant insolence would have disappointed your mother."

His comment was designed to fill Miyuki with shame, but it failed.

You don't know how Mother talked about you when you weren't around, she thought. *"The grayer his hair, the smaller his mind." That's what she said about you.*

Her father turned right around and stood with his back to his daughter.

This was an old trick. It used to work, making her beg for his forgiveness.

Now she just thought, *Good. Lecture's over.*

He stood like that for a full two minutes. Miyuki timed it by the clock on the gymnasium wall. For those two minutes, she was the silent daughter he said he always wanted.

He finally gave up waiting for an apology and walked away, taking great care to keep his back to her as he went. This was a challenge, as he had to zigzag around tables, cots and clumps of people.

The earthquake that had changed all their lives shook Japan as far away as Tokyo. It opened up the ground under the ocean and sent a huge wave to swallow the land. It set off explosions at the Fukushima nuclear power plant, and radiation escaped into the environment. The government ordered everyone to leave the danger zone, twenty kilometers around the plant.

"You still whining about that stupid donkey?"

Tani, her fourteen-year-old brother, left the chessboard where he had just been defeated by his friend Yoshi. (*Too easily*, Miyuki thought. She had seen the board. She could have checkmated Yoshi in five moves.)

Tani sat beside her on the tatami.

"Shut up," she said. "You don't care."

"What's the point of caring?" he asked. "No point."

Miyuki knew her brother would not say such things if their mother was with them.

If their mother was with them, he wouldn't want to.

But their mother was swimming in the sea, a long, long swim. A five-day swim now, and counting. They all watched the water, waiting for her to come kicking her way to shore, buoyed up by part of someone's roof or clinging to a board that used to be a piece of someone's floor.

"She's probably dead by now anyway," said Tani.

"Who?"

"That stupid donkey. Who do you think I'm talking about?"

"Don't you want to know for sure?"

"Don't care," said Tani. "She's an animal. She's down here." He put his hand two feet from the floor. "Man is up here." He reached for the sky. "Girls are down here." He put his hand flat to the floor and squished it down, trying to go even lower.

"You're a chauvinist pig," Miyuki said. "No. I take that back. That's an insult to pigs. You're just a chauvinist."

Tani laughed, but it was a hard laugh, without humor.

"You care about that donkey so much, go and get it. Stop talking about it. All you do is talk."

Miyuki looked at her brother. He was crying again. He cried easily these days.

"You won't go, will you?" he said meanly. "You won't go, and you won't stop talking about it. You make me sick." He shoved her, hard. "Get away from me. Go sit with the old ladies. Go sit with the babies. Go anywhere. I don't care."

Miyuki could have argued with him. Being two years older did not give him the right to talk to her like that. But everything he said was true.

She got up off the mat and walked away.

It was not easy to cross the gym. Evacuees were everywhere. Some were on cots with their eyes closed, trying to sleep even though the lights were on and it was only nine o'clock at night. Some were playing cards or dominoes or just talking.

People gathered around tables piled high with donated clothing. They looked over the snack tables for something to eat or drink. Children ran around where they could find space to run, tired of being scared and away from home. Volunteers in orange vests brought diapers to mothers, blankets to old people and gave presentations on signs of radiation poisoning.

"You might feel very weak and tired," a volunteer said, holding up a poster with information on it. "You might have an upset stomach or a headache. You might notice that your hair is falling out. Be sure to take your potassium iodine to protect your thyroid."

Miyuki had heard this information so many times she could recite it from memory.

She finally found a place to sit near the back of the gym. She hugged her school bag to her chest, wishing she could hug her mother instead. But she didn't know where her mother was.

She knew where her mother's donkey was, but she was not brave enough to go there.

Miyuki had never gone anywhere by herself. Her mother drove her to school or shopping or anywhere else she needed to go. The evacuation center was five kilometers outside the danger zone. Her home was eight kilometers inside the danger zone. How could she walk all that way?

It was a thing she might do in her head, but she would never do it in real life. That was not who she was.

She was a girl who complained — a little — and asked questions — a few. But she was mostly a girl who did what people expected.

"This is who I am," she whispered to the floor. "Tani is right."

The words were bitter to her. The sound of them made her mad.

"My brother doesn't get to decide who I am!" she said. "My father does not get to decide who I am!"

What if, she thought. *What if I put some water in my school bag?*

She and Hisa would both need clean water to drink. There were many bottles in the hall. The volunteers regularly urged the evacuees to "Drink, drink!" Miyuki had as much right to that water as anyone.

It would be a simple matter to act in this small way.

"Will I do it?" she whispered. "Is this who I am?"

Miyuki stood. She went to one of the tables full of water and put four bottles into her school bag, then added two more. Hisa would be thirsty. She moved to the snack table and added packs of Senbei rice crackers, steam buns filled with red bean paste and three apples.

No one paid any attention to her as she moved through the crowded gym and walked out of the school. Small groups of volunteers and evacuees sat on the front steps watching the moon rise over the bay below. Miyuki tiptoed across the porch and went softly down the stairs at the side. She walked across the parking lot. The street took her up a hill and around a bend.

After almost an hour of walking, Miyuki got to the end of the safe zone. Across the street, a low wooden barrier with flashing lights and a Keep Out sign marked the beginning of the danger zone.

Miyuki looked across the road at the barrier she needed to cross. No cars were coming. There was no one else in sight.

She took a deep breath of safe air, then ran across the street. She ducked under the Keep Out sign. She held the safe air in her lungs as long as she could, but before long she had to exhale, then breathe in again.

The dangerous air seemed the same as the safe air.

Miyuki kept walking.

She walked on streets she'd driven on with her family, through villages she'd known all her life. The electricity was off. The only lights working were the solar-powered ones.

The silence was eerie. She stomped her shoes on the sidewalk just to give herself something to listen to.

She passed shops with no customers and a railway station with no passengers. She left the sidewalk and walked down the middle of the street, just because she could, and because it gave her some distance from the shrubs in people's gardens. In the moonlight, they looked a bit like ghosts.

A soft rain began to fall. It picked up intensity

and Miyuki responded by picking up the speed of her steps.

The rain will wash away the radiation, she thought. Then she wondered if she was right about that.

By the time she arrived in her village, she was in a deluge. She was totally soaked when she turned into her street.

Miyuki did not care. She started to run.

Would Hisa still be there? Would she have gotten out somehow and be lost now?

The worst thing would be if Hisa was there, but dead.

Miyuki ran to her house, up the driveway and across the backyard. She saw the donkey pen in the corner with its small three-walled shelter.

At first she could not see her mother's donkey. It was too dark in the yard, and the rain in her eyes made it hard to see anything.

"Hisa?" she yelled. "Are you there?"

Miyuki threw herself at the pen. Now she could see the outline of the animal crouched in a corner of the shelter. In seconds she was inside the pen and down by the donkey's side.

Hisa raised her head and put it in Miyuki's lap. Miyuki opened a bottle of water and tipped it into the donkey's mouth. Hisa drank it like a baby, and then she ate the apple Miyuki gave her.

"Can you walk?" Miyuki asked. Hisa got to her feet. Miyuki looped a rope loosely around the donkey's neck and they left the pen.

She looked up at her house. It was dark and looked abandoned. She realized she'd been hoping her mother would be there, but there was no one.

She led Hisa out of the yard and down the street.

The rain eased off to a drizzle. Miyuki's legs and feet were sore beyond sore. One step, then another. She kept going.

They were passing the empty train station when Miyuki heard the sound of something running up behind her. She spun around to see a small white dog. It stepped back when it got close to her and whimpered.

"Where did you come from?" Miyuki asked. "Do you want to come with us?" She poured some water into her hand and the little dog lapped it up. "Come on, then."

The little dog barked. Miyuki heard another dog bark in reply. She followed the sound and found a larger dog, a black one, tied to a tree.

"Don't be afraid," she imagined her mother saying. Miyuki shared a steam bun between the two dogs and poured out more water for them. She untied the rope from the tree, and the four of them moved through the empty streets.

Hisa was nervous about the dogs at first, but she trusted Miyuki and kept on walking.

The next time Miyuki turned around, two more dogs had joined them.

"Are you sending them to me?" Miyuki called up to heaven. She felt her mother smiling at her.

The dogs and the donkey were good company. The walk back seemed shorter with friends to share it.

The sky was now more gray than black. Morning was coming. Miyuki had walked all night.

She knew the barrier was coming up. Soon after that, she would be back at the evacuation center.

She wondered if anyone would be happy to see her.

"Maybe I'll be arrested for breaking the rules." She scratched Hisa between her ears and decided she didn't care if she was.

"I am someone who rescues animals," she said.

"I am someone who walks a long way, alone, at night, and in the rain. I am someone my mother would be proud of. This is who I am."

She rounded the bend and was met by bright lights on the other side of the barrier.

"There she is!"

That was her father's voice.

"I see her. She's all right!"

That was her brother's.

Miyuki heard the crowd cheering behind the lights. They were cheering for her! As she got closer, the dogs ran ahead, jumping into the arms of the people who'd had to leave them behind.

The police pushed aside the barrier for Miyuki and Hisa to go through.

"Stand back," the police said. "She needs to be decontaminated."

Tani and her father ignored the warning. Tani was crying. He threw his arms around the donkey.

Miyuki's father was crying. He bent down to hug her.

"You are just like your mother, Miyuki," he said, holding her close. "You are just like your mother."

Call me Nariko, she thought, with her face pressed against her father's jacket.

I am thunder.

8

The Freedom Chair

Day One

Mike is sitting on his heels on the floor of his cell.

His head is bent low. His hands are pulled tight behind him. He is weighed down by the pressure of a knee pressing into the small of his back and by four men leaning into him. It is hard for him to breathe.

"Keep your hands behind your back! Head down! Don't move until you hear the door shut!"

One by one, Mike feels the corrections officers loosen their grip on him and back away. The last one, Knee-in-Back, uses his knee like a fist to give

Mike an extra poke in the kidney. Then he, too, gets off him and the cell door slams shut.

Mike does not move a muscle. He stays as he was placed while the COs congratulate themselves and laugh.

Mike hears the outer door of the Administrative Segregation pod shut and lock.

He is all alone.

He flops over onto his side, draws his knees up to his chest, buries his face and silently cries.

Just for a moment. Then he bounces to his feet, ready for whatever might come next. His eyes are wiped and his face is dry by the time he hears the Ad Seg door unlock again and the peephole covering in his own door slide open.

"You all right in there, 75293?"

Mike knows the voice of CO Jenson. It is the voice of the devil.

Mike does not answer.

"Don't go crazy in there, y'hear?" CO Jenson taunts. Then he slides the peephole door shut again and rejoins his buddies.

"Don't go crazy," Mike whispers. "Don't become like you, you mean."

He keeps his voice low.

"Don't talk in Seg," the boys in his cell block told him, sharing their stories of how tough they were. "They'll mace you if you do. The only ones who talk in Seg are the ones who've gone bat-strapped loony, and they scream more than they talk."

Mike looks around his new cell, which takes all of five seconds.

There is a concrete slab for a bed. It has a thin rubber mattress that smells like pee and disinfectant. There is a metal toilet with a small sink on the top of it. One roll of toilet paper sits on a small shelf. There is one gray blanket. These are the only things in the room.

"Sixty-seven days," Mike whispers. He wonders if this day counts as one, or if the count doesn't start until tomorrow.

Sixty-seven days.

Sixty-seven days.

Sixty-seven days.

Day Two

The flap at the bottom of the cell door clangs open.

"Grub," someone says.

Mike spent a long night trying to sleep. At least he thinks it was night. The lights stayed on so he couldn't be sure. Now he is having trouble sitting up.

"Hurry up, inmate. I got others to feed."

The voice is more boy than man. There is something young about it. Mike bends low and takes the covered plastic tray from the shelf in the door.

The face of another inmate, an older boy, looks back at him. The older boy winks.

"Be cool," the boy whispers.

"Do I have to come in there?" yells a CO.

The flap is closed and the Ad Seg pod door shuts soon after.

Mike takes the tray to his bed, then changes his mind and sits on the floor. He is hungry! He got no food yesterday because he was in the chow line when he got thrown into Seg.

"We're in apple country," he said when a scoop of canned applesauce was plopped down on his tray. "It's harvest time. Real apples are cheap right now."

"What's that, inmate?" asked CO Jenson, barreling up to the conversation. "Are you complaining about the food the taxpayers have provided to feed your sorry self?"

"I'm just saying, you can buy a bushel of seconds for a couple of bucks. The taxpayers pay less and we could have real apples. There's no food value in canned applesauce."

He knows this because his mom told him. He also knows it is dead easy to make good applesauce from real apples because he's done it, but he didn't get the chance to say that because Jenson slammed his fist on Mike's tray, sending it crashing to the floor.

When Mike said, "Hey!" the COs swarmed in and hauled him to Ad Seg.

Fifteen days for spreading dissention.

Fifteen days for the "Hey!"

Fourteen days for saying two curse words when the COs knocked him down.

Fifteen days for speaking without first being spoken to.

Eight days for making a mess when his tray got knocked away.

Sixty-seven days.

Mike already spent time yesterday wondering why two curse words were worth less time than one single "Hey!" and decided that this was a puzzle that could not be solved.

He is so hungry now that even the canned applesauce will taste delicious.

He takes off the tray cover and wants to be sick.

On the tray is one item. It is round, like a burger, and smells like feet.

He covers it up and pushes it away.

Then he eats it. He almost throws up, but he doesn't.

Day Three

"Are you crazy yet?" Jenson asks through the peephole. "Don't worry. You'll get there."

Mike rises from his bed like a superhero and throws himself at the closed door so fast Jenson doesn't have time to step back from it.

Jenson curses, then spits out, "You better not have damaged that door, inmate!"

Mike braces for a beating but Jenson remains outside the cell and, seconds later, retreats behind the Ad Seg pod door.

Mike stays on the floor, his shoulder hurting where it slammed into the metal. He smiles. One for him. He'll pay for it later, he is sure, but for now, it's something good.

Across the room in a spot he hasn't noticed before, a previous tenant has scratched part of a curse word into the wall. The first letter is deep and clear. The second letter is only half-finished.

"Probably a U," Mike whispers.

Maybe it isn't a swear word. Maybe the writer was trying to write FUN.

Right.

Day Five

Another day, another tray, another ground-up boot to eat.

Mike sits facing his door so that he has a chance to see the face of the inmate bringing him his meal.

He misses faces. He never thought about faces until he couldn't see them anymore. He misses darkness, too. He never thought about darkness until he was stuck under bright fluorescent lights glaring down at him twenty-four hours a day.

The outer door of the pod opens, then Mike's food slot opens.

The face of the older boy stares back at him.

"You staying cool?" the boy whispers, sliding the meal tray into place.

"I'm not going to make it," Mike whispers back.

"You are," the inmate says. "Use what you have. Free your head."

The CO yells. The inmate closes the meal-slot flap and Mike is left alone with his foot-burger.

"Use what I have?" asks Mike. "I've got nothing. Nothing!"

He kicks the tray across the floor. The tray cover comes off and Mike sees something new.

Along with the foot-burger, the tray holds two small packets of ketchup.

The red against the gray of the cell looks like all the flowers in the world.

One packet is enough to mask the taste of the chopped boot. The second packet goes under the mattress, a feast for another day.

"Use what I have," Mike says.

He starts to really think about what he has.

Day Seven

Mike stares at the sky. So blue! So beautiful! He breathes deeply of the fresh air. He fills his lungs.

"Move, inmate," yells CO Jenson. "It's large-muscle exercise time, so move those large muscles or I'll move them for you."

The exercise cage is not much larger than his cell, but without the concrete bunk taking up half of it, it feels enormous. Plus, there is wire mesh instead of walls. Mike runs from corner to corner, bounces off the fence and keeps on running. He does the things he learned to do in gym class. He runs to one end, drops to the ground, runs to the other end, drops to the ground. He notices Jenson has his back to him. Mike scoops up gravel from the floor of the cage. He hides what he finds in his jumpsuit pocket and just keeps running.

Day Ten

"Pawn to king's bishop seven," Mike says as he looks down at the chessboard. He makes his move, then he gets up, goes to the other side of the board and becomes his opponent, assessing the battle from this new point of view.

What he has. Toilet paper and water to mold into chess pieces that took two days to dry. A dab of ketchup turned half the pieces pink. One of the pebbles he picked up in the yard etched a chessboard into the cell floor. Memories of being in fourth-grade chess club reminded him how to play.

He plays chess for hours. He takes on different opponents. One time he plays Wolverine. Another time he takes on the ghost of Prince. He thinks of playing against God but figures God would have too much of an advantage, so he plays against Batman instead.

Day Seventeen

There is a mini chocolate bar on his tray with the foot-burger. Someone has given up their commissary.

Mike nibbles at it in small insect-sized bites, making it last and last.

Day Twenty-three

"Taxpayers paid for that toilet paper to use in the proper way, not for you to waste! Five more days in Seg for that."

They make him sweep away his chess set, his papier-mâché marbles and a sculpture he was trying to make of the Incredible Hulk. The COs are supposed to take him out for a shower, but they don't.

Mike slumps in a corner. His back hurts in this position, but he doesn't have the will to change it.

Day Twenty-eight

Mike stops eating. The foot-patties go back to the kitchen untouched. No one asks if he is ill.

Day Thirty-two

Mike wakes up in the infirmary, chained to the bed, an IV drip feeding into his arm.

"You almost left us," the nurse says. "Don't you like the nutritional loaf? It's got everything in it your body needs to survive."

Mike doesn't answer. He doesn't even look at her.

His time in the infirmary doesn't count toward his punishment. The doctor declares him healthy and he's put back in his Ad Seg cell.

It's been Day Thirty-two for four days.

Day Forty

They check now to make sure he eats.

"Had a kid in the hole die on them once," Jenson says through the peephole. "No one knew it for three days. Load of paperwork on that one. Now I have to watch you eat."

Mike doesn't care enough to talk back. He puts the food tray on the floor by the closed door and takes off the cover.

There is a book on the tray, a ratty old Agatha Christie novel called *Murder on the Orient Express*.

Mike silently places the book on the floor where the CO can't see it from the peephole. Mike picks up the foot-patty, steps out in front of the peephole and chows down on it. He wiggles his tongue to show he swallowed it, then he slides the tray back out through the slot. Jenson leaves without comment.

Mike opens the book.

Someone has written a message on the inside cover. Maybe for him, maybe for someone else.

You are not alone.

Mike shuts the book and hugs it to his chest.

Other people have been held in cells like this one, held in even worse cells. Nelson Mandela. Gandhi. Jesus. Those women who wanted to vote. Muhammad Ali. The guy who carved the F and part of a second letter into the wall of this cell.

They did it.

He can do it.

He opens the book and lets it take him on a long, long train ride.

Day Sixty-three

Mike is doing a wall sit. He's been alternating wall sits to a count of three hundred with pushups and jumping jacks.

He'll exercise his large muscle groups when *he* feels like it, not just when Jenson tells him to.

From his position on the wall he stares straight at the half-written curse word.

Maybe it's not supposed to be a curse word, he thinks. Maybe the guy was trying to write his name. Maybe what he thinks is half a U is really an O, for a name like Ford or ...

Mike can't think of any other name that begins with F-O.

Maybe it's not a name but a word. Not a curse word. A regular word, like FOSSIL. Maybe the kid felt like he was being buried in here.

Or he could have been writing FORGET.

Forget what? Forget his past? Forget his punishment? Did the kid want people to forget him?

Mike comes down off his wall sit and crouches beside the half word.

"Could be FORGIVE, too," he says, and he sits with that thought for a bit.

"What will the next kid want to see?" he quietly asks the room. "What will help him?"

FORGIVE might sound like a command from a social worker or a Bible thumper.

Suddenly Mike knows what word will be right, if he can do it.

The small stones he's picked up from the exercise cage now line the wall of his cell, blending into the gray of the floor. He picks one up and starts carving.

FORWARD

Day Seventy-two
"Move out," orders Jenson.

Mike moves out.

He doesn't look back.

Day Seventeen Out of Seg
Mike is working in the prison kitchen. He's new at it and he has a lot to learn. He washes a lot of trays. He peels a lot of potatoes. He follows a lot of orders.

"We got a new kid in the hole," the kitchen chief calls out. "Heat up a loaf."

Mike's stomach heaves at the sight of the foot-patty being lifted out of the freezer and tossed in the microwave.

He swallows hard. He has been waiting for this moment.

He moves from the sink to the counter where the microwave sits. When the oven finishes, he places the hot punishment loaf on a tray, taking care not to breathe in the stench.

With a quick look over his shoulder, he takes the Agatha Christie novel out of one pocket and a small pack of red licorice from his commissary order out of the other. The lid goes on the tray and the tray goes off to the hole.

"You're not alone," he whispers to the unknown boy.

Forward.

9

The Hiding Chair

Noosala was sitting on a mat.

The landlord called it a carpet.

"Be sure to keep that carpet clean," he said nearly every time he came into the apartment. "If those babies spit up on that nice carpet, I'm going to have to charge you extra."

That last bit was a ridiculous threat. The landlord already knew he had taken almost all the money they had.

Besides, this was not a carpet.

A carpet was something made in the shacks of Afghanistan, hung on frames and tied with the small hands of women and children who breathed in the fibers and whose backs got stiff and sore from hours of cramped sitting.

A carpet was a sturdy, luxurious thing. A carpet was strong enough to be washed in a river and dried on a rock, thick enough to feel smooth on rough ground and soft enough to cover the back of a horse.

A baby was no threat to a real Afghan carpet!

This thing that Noosala sat on was flat and plastic. It was horrid. It was not a carpet.

Noosala knew. She had woven carpets all her life.

"We could ask the landlord to set up a carpet frame for us," she said out loud without thinking. She spoke quietly, though. Her voice automatically stayed quiet now. Even the little ones hardly ever cried louder than a whisper.

"You want us to make him a carpet?" Aunt Freyba asked her. "You want us to break our backs and cut up our fingers to make something beautiful for *him*? I suppose you think he will go sell this carpet and bring us back the money. Is that what you think?"

Noosala's aunt used to be fun. In the good days, before the war, the family saw her twice a year.

She brought them presents like dolls and change purses she had made from clothing scraps and told them funny stories about when she and Mama were little girls.

Now Mama and Papa were dead and Aunt Freyba was just foul.

"After all, the landlord has been so trustworthy so far," Aunt Freyba said. "He has gotten us to safety, hasn't he? We are all living a grand new life, aren't we? We are eating too much food every day, aren't we? Are you thinking we owe him money for all the fabulous food he brings us? Do you think we owe him money, you silly girl? Is that what you think?"

Many, many times, Noosala wished she never again had to hear that phrase — "Is that what you think?"

Their landlord was the same man who had smuggled them out of Afghanistan. Noosala's father had found him for the group through one of his neighbors in Mazar-e-Sharif. The group would have blamed her father for their misery, but he was arrested at an unexpected Taliban checkpoint as they were heading out of the country. The Taliban shot him right in front of Noosala.

"The rest of you — go!" the checkpoint commander ordered. Aunt Freyba forced Noosala back into the truck. She had to leave her father in the dust, unburied.

"I will care for you," Aunt Freyba said then. "I will be your mother and your father, and you will be my child."

Noosala's mother died of pneumonia back in Mazar, and Aunt Freyba's family was killed in a rocket attack.

Noosala allowed herself to be held in Freyba's arms — she was too upset to pull away — but she remembered her father's warnings at the start of the trip.

"Do not trust Freyba. The war has made her mean," he said. "And don't tell anyone about your gold. Not ever."

Sure enough, two days into their journey, Aunt Freyba said to her, "Give me your gold. I'll hang on to it. It will be safer with me."

"I have no gold, Auntie," Noosala lied. "It all went to pay for medicine for my mother."

"But your mother's ring. Her earrings. What about those?"

"That's all the gold there was, and it's gone."

"All of it?"

"All of it, Auntie."

Freyba pulled away from her then. Noosala blessed her father for his advice.

"My turn to sit with my back to the wall," Aunt Freyba declared, getting to her feet and kicking at Noosala to move. "You're so eager to weave carpets, you won't mind sitting with nothing to prop up your back."

Noosala didn't listen for anyone to defend her. She knew no one would. There were eighteen other people cooped up in this room.

In the early days, everyone worked together, trying to make it as easy as possible for everyone else. They helped out with each other's children and passed the time sharing stories. Being out of reach of the Taliban meant they could relax a little, and everyone slept a great deal.

Eight months in, they had shared all their stories, and patience was as low as their supply of food.

The men decided they needed their own space away from the women and children, so they divided the room with hanging blankets, keeping the larger half for themselves. They had more wall space to lean against. They had more room to stretch out and could even exercise a little, if they did it quietly.

The women and children's section of the room was chopped up with the bathroom and the kitchen shelves. It did not have much wall space. They had to take turns.

Noosala moved as far away from everyone as she could, which was only about four feet. This put her right against the kitchen shelves.

"Move away from there!" the oldest woman, Spurghai, said. "You'll break my bowl! It's all I have left of my house. Make her move! She'll break it!"

Noosala was nowhere near the old lady's bowl, but she stood up anyway. There was nowhere left for her to sit except in the tiny lavatory, and some-one else was there now.

Noosala took two steps to the window and pre-tended to look outside.

If I could just see the sun again, she thought.

"Stay away from the window!" the landlord said over and over. "Don't touch the drapes. There are police right outside, watching for illegals like you. If they see you, they'll ship you right back to the Taliban."

For eight months, the heavy green, dusty drapes kept the room dark at night and dim during the day.

Maybe I could hide under the drapes, Noosala thought. *I could make them into a cave, like I did when I was a child.*

She could not remember the last time she had been alone.

She heard the sound of someone coming up the stairs.

All nineteen of them clustered around the door. The landlord was coming!

The key turned in the lock. The landlord came in carrying a bag. One bag.

"Don't crowd me," he snarled. Then he sneezed. One, two, three sneezes followed by a long bout of coughing

"Is this all you've brought?" asked Sayed Ali, the oldest man. "You have not been here for a week. We have been out of food since yesterday."

"Yeah, well, now you have some. It stinks in here."

"You promised us soap."

"Soap costs money." The landlord sneezed again and bent over in another fit of coughing.

"Ungrateful dogs. No 'Thank you for coming here when you are sick.' All you want is more, more, more."

"All we want are the visas you promised us, the visas we paid for. We have been in this room for eight months. The children have not seen the sun for eight months!"

"No sunburn, then, right?" the landlord said. "There's a problem with the visas. I need more money."

"More? We've given you so much."

"And you've eaten so much. Come on. I see some rings, some watches. Hand them over." His words were punctuated by loud, hacking coughs.

Slowly, reluctantly, watches, rings and brooches were placed in the landlord's hands.

Noosala did not move. Her gold remained hidden, sewn into the hem of her skirt. Her mother's ring and earrings belonged to her. They were all she had in the world, and she was not going to give them up, especially since she did not think for a moment that she would get a visa in exchange.

"Don't look at me like I am a bad guy," said the landlord. "I have gone to considerable trouble for you people. And for what? For you to look at

me like I'm a thief? I won't put up with that." He
pocketed their jewelry. "If you are not happy with
these arrangements, leave. Go outside. Take your
chances with the Uzbek police. The amount of
rent I could get for this flat! I ought to turn you
over to the police myself."

"No, no," Sayed Ali said. Noosala would not
have bothered. The landlord had made these
threats before. "We know this is a hardship for you
as well. We are just tired of waiting."

"That's what life is," said the landlord, sneezing
as he handed the bag over to Sayed Ali. "Waiting
to die. We are all just waiting to die. Me, I'm going
home to wait in my bed. Don't bother thanking
me."

Before he left, he reminded them, "Don't touch
those drapes! Keep those kids away from those
windows." He coughed some more, then left the
flat. They heard him turn the key to lock them
inside.

The bag held three loaves of bread, a small tub
of margarine and a small jar of honey.

Ali handed it to the women.

"Feed the little ones first," he said.

Noosala knew that by the time the small children ate and then the men ate, there would be next to nothing left for her.

The women got busy. They had a task to do. They had to divide up the bread and honey. They went to the task with full gusto, each one of them wanting a piece of the work. It was something to do.

Noosala woke up with an empty belly. By the end of the next day, flu gripped the noses and bellies of the smallest and the oldest. The stench rose with their fevers.

Soon half the flat was ill.

I'm going to go mad, Noosala thought. *I'm going to go mad and then I am going to die in this terrible room.*

Noosala tried to bury that thought in work. She rinsed and washed as well as she could without soap, wiping down the feverish ones with cool cloths and trying to keep them covered.

She was not sick. Everyone else, it seemed, was.

I'll be the last, she thought. *I'll work to make everyone better. Then they will get well and I'll get sick. They will go on to Europe and they will leave me here to die.*

Still, she kept working to care for the others. There was nothing else to do.

It wasn't enough. Within days, death came for Sayed Ali and for old Spurghai and for Aunt Freyba.

The littlest ones were in a really bad way, too.

"We need a doctor," Noosala said. She stared at the door, waiting for the landlord to walk through it. "We need medicine. We can't all just wait to die."

And we need to get rid of the bodies, she thought, trying not to look into the corner where the three dead bodies were under a blanket.

"What are we going to do?" she asked the room, and no one answered her.

"Never touch the drapes," the landlord had warned them over and over. "Never look out the window. There is a police station right across the street. They will see your foreign faces and they will throw you in a dungeon, even the children. They will beat you and torture you and ship you back to the Taliban. Stay away from the windows!"

They had stayed away. They had stayed quiet. For eight long months they had stayed quiet and hungry and obedient, while the landlord took their money and kept them prisoner in this dismal place.

Now they had no more money, three of them were dead and more would be dead soon.

If Noosala stayed in this room, she would die a silent, desperate, lonely death. If she left, she would probably die a screaming, painful death, either at the hands of the Uzbek police or at the hands of the Taliban.

Or maybe not.

Maybe she would live. Maybe she would ride a great train of suffering for a long, long time, but there might be one day when that train would stop, and she could have a belly full of food and a face full of sun.

I want to live, Noosala thought.

She stepped up to the window. She took hold of the drapes. She yanked them open.

Behind her she heard moans and a feeble "What are you doing?" But no one was strong enough now to stop her.

The bright light hurt her eyes. She blinked the pain away and looked out the window.

There was no police station across the street. There were no police on the sidewalks. All she saw were small apartment buildings and children playing marbles.

Noosala banged on the window. The children looked up.

"Help!" she screamed in Pashtun. "Help us!"

She waved her arms.

The children went back to their game. She yelled and banged and waved until they looked up again.

The children on the sidewalk huddled together in quick conversation. They gathered up their marbles. Two ran into one of the houses. The other two ran toward Noosala's building.

Soon there was banging on the door and children were calling out in a language Noosala didn't know. The children's voices were joined by other, older voices, and then Noosala heard the sound of the lock being broken.

Strangers rushed into the room, stunned at the sight of the sick and the dead.

"I can work," Noosala said in Pashtun, even though it was clear they could not understand her. "I can look after children and clean and cook and weave carpets and do any kind of work you want me to do." She went from stranger to stranger, appealing to them for help.

The strangers looked too overwhelmed and too bewildered to know what to do with her or with any of the others who were coughing and vomiting on the plastic rug.

A policeman came through the door. He took one look at the room, then spoke quickly into his radio.

Help was coming. Or pain was coming.

Death was coming. Or life was coming.

Noosala decided not to wait.

In the middle of the confusion of people arriving and people being carried out, Noosala slipped by herself down the stairs and out the door of the building.

She breathed in her first fresh air in eight months.

Then she walked.

She did not look back.

10
The War Chair

Sue was sitting on a swing.

She dangled her feet loosely over the gravel below and moved herself idly back and forth as if she didn't care. She watched the ground appear to move beneath her feet.

"Suey, I am talking to you," Mom said. "Don't just sit there. Give me some sign that you hear me."

"She hears you," said Barry, Sue's older brother. He was on the swing next to hers but he wasn't swinging. He was sitting bone-still, which was not all that easy to do on a swing. "The whole town hears you," he muttered.

Sue wanted to giggle but she didn't.

"Do we really need your lip today?" Mom asked Barry. "I'm trying to make this easy for you. Do you think this is easy for me? It wouldn't hurt you to help me for a change."

"Don't put this on me!" Barry snapped back. "I didn't make you and Dad fight all the time."

Their mom got to arguing with Barry and left Sue alone.

Sue really wanted to swing. She wanted to pump her legs and push with her back and make the swing move high and fast so that she could feel the air whoosh around her.

Mom was in the way. She stood in front of them, just enough on Barry's side and just enough on Sue's side to make it impossible for either of them to swing.

"I hope you're not going to go in there with that snippy attitude," their mother said to Barry.

Sue cringed at the word "snippy." She knew Barry hated it, too. It wasn't right that Mom was tossing it around today, this very strange day.

Their mother really wasn't being fair to Barry.

Just that morning, between mouthfuls of corn-flakes, Barry had whispered to Sue, "This isn't my fault, is it?"

I don't know, Sue had thought. *I don't know any-thing.* But she looked right at him and shook her head. Then she opened her mouth at him to show him all the mashed-up cornflakes in there.

It made him laugh and earned her a "Quit fool-ing around" from their mother.

"I'm sure it's a nice place," Mom said now. She fished through her purse, looking for a cigarette.

"You quit," Sue said. "Remember?"

"Picked a damn fool time to do that," their mother said to herself, sighing as she closed her purse.

"Better late than never," Barry said, which got him a Mom-frown, even though Sue knew he meant it as a compliment. Barry sometimes said the wrong words when he was nervous.

Mom checked her watch. "I guess we'd better go in. Come on. Stand up. Let me look at you."

Sue and Barry stepped off their swings. Mom slicked back Barry's hair and pulled up Sue's left knee sock, which had slipped down around her ankle.

"I know you're scared, but it's going to be all right," their mother said. "If they ask you how you are, you tell them you are fine. If your father asks how you are, you tell him the same thing. Tell him I'm fine, too, if he asks."

"He won't ask," Sue said.

They left the swings and walked across the dirt yard to the low building next to the parking lot. The sign on the building read *Family Mediation and Supervised Visitation Service*.

Mom opened the door. "Let's go."

I don't want to go in there, Sue thought.

She backed away from the door.

"Suey, I said, let's go! Your father will be here in a moment and I'm not supposed to be around when he gets here. You want me to get in trouble with the court? Is that what you want? Get inside."

"I don't want to."

"Who wants to?" Mom took Sue's hand to pull her along.

Sue sat down, right on the sidewalk. It was a stunt she vaguely remembered doing when she was younger and being forced into something she didn't want to do, like go to bed.

The ground seemed a lot farther down than it did when she was three.

"Are you kidding me?" her mother asked. "Suey, you are six years old!"

"Seven," said Barry.

Their mother shot Barry a quick glare, then turned back to Sue.

"You look absolutely foolish sitting there," Mom said. "Well, I'm not going to force you. I'm not going to carry you in. That's all I need, to have someone see me fighting with you. Barry, go get somebody. Tell them that Sue doesn't want to see her father."

"I want to see Daddy!" Sue protested. She started to cry. Why was everything so hard?

"Who am I supposed to get?" Barry asked. "I don't know anybody in there."

Mom went inside the building. Barry stood over Sue, watching her cry.

Do something! Susan begged him with her thoughts. She did not want to keep crying and sitting on the sidewalk, but she did not know what else to do.

Barry sat down on the sidewalk beside her.

A middle-aged man with a big middle walked by carrying a plastic bag full of stuff from the Bulk Barn. He stared at Sue and her brother as he passed.

"Dogs sit on the ground," he said.

"What did you say?" Barry yelled at him. "You calling us dogs? Get over here and say that. We'll bite your face off. Yeah, coward, just keep walking. Go home and fill your face with Crunchy Munchies or Hungry Hippie or whatever it is you've got in that bag. Keep moving! Run! *RUN!*"

But the Bulk Barn man was already way down the street.

"Hungry Hippie," Sue laughed. Then she hiccuped. Her nose was running. She didn't have a tissue. She was going to use her hand but Barry tore a leaf from a hosta plant in the garden and gave it to her to use instead.

"Careful, it's poison ivy," Barry said as she cleaned her face with it.

Sue just grinned. She knew it wasn't poison ivy. She held the soiled leaf out to him.

"*I* don't want it."

"What do I do with it?"

They looked around.

"Put it through the mail slot," Barry suggested. She did, and she knew it was the wrong thing to do but it felt like absolutely the right thing to do.

"Let's get this dumb thing over with," Barry said.

"It is dumb," Sue agreed. They went inside.

No one had told Sue what to expect, so she had made up what she thought the family center would look like. She thought it would be like a doctor's office, and also like a principal's office, and also like church.

It was like none of those things and it was like all of those things.

There was a big desk like a principal would have. There were filing cabinets along the wall like a doctor's office would have. And there was a feeling of hushness and seriousness like in church. There were also a few old sofas, a low table full of little-kid toys, shelves with books and games like Monopoly and another shelf with coloring books and crayons.

A door with a picture of Superwoman on it opened and their mother came out, drying her eyes. She was followed by an old woman in a long, full skirt and a rainbow-colored blouse that seemed to fluff out in all directions.

Mom bent down to Sue and Barry. "Your father will be here soon. I have to go. This is Ms. Dira. She will look after you until he gets here. Be good for Daddy. Or don't. I don't care."

Rainbow woman coughed a little.

Mom looked at her, then said, "Behave yourselves at your father's house. Have a good time. I'll see you in two days."

She hugged them both quickly and left.

Sue sighed deeply. Part one of this strange day was over. Part two was on now — dealing with this funny-looking lady. Part three would be with Daddy. She and Barry hadn't seen him since he moved out three weeks ago.

Would he look different? Would he still like them? Where would she sleep at his house? Would he remember how to make them supper? Did he remember she didn't like peas?

Ms. Dira smiled at them and opened her mouth to say something, but she was interrupted by shouting from outside.

Barry ran to the window, Sue right behind him.

Their father had arrived and their mother had not yet left. The two of them were in the parking lot screaming at each other. They slapped the cars.

They stomped away, then turned back for more yelling.

"This is their war," said Ms. Dira, who was standing behind Sue and her brother. She put one hand on Sue's shoulder and another one on Barry's. "This is their war, not yours. This is their choice, not yours."

She led them away from the window and they all sat together around the low table.

"My parents fought all the time," she said. It was hard for Sue to imagine that someone with so many wrinkles ever had parents. "I had to find something that I liked, that was just for me. Otherwise I would have disappeared into their fights."

"What did you find?" Sue asked.

The old lady giggled and looked from side to side as if there were spies all around that were eager to learn her secret. Then she reached into her skirt pocket and pulled out a small cloth bag. She opened the drawstring and emptied the contents of the bag into the palm of her hand.

"Marbles," Ms. Dira said. "I like marbles."

"Marbles?" Sue asked.

"When I was a little girl, I had a marble collection that I kept in an old cigar box under my bed,"

Ms. Dira said. "Whenever my parents fought, I took out my collection and looked at it and played with it and I felt better."

"You still like marbles?" Barry asked. "For real?"

"For real," said Ms. Dira. "I love the shape of them, the colors, the feel, the things I can do with them — everything! I love them so much that I became an expert. As a matter of fact, I am one of the leading marble experts in the world right now! Did you know that the ancient Egyptians made marbles? Lots of civilizations had them."

Ms. Dira talked a bit more about marbles. Then she asked Sue, "What does your brother love to do?"

"Barry watches people," she said. Barry looked shocked, but of course she knew that! "He is very curious about other people."

"Barry might take that curiosity and use it to become a writer. Or maybe a psychologist, someone who tries to figure out why people do the things they do. Maybe he will become a detective and solve mysteries. Barry, what does your sister love to do?"

"Sizes," Barry said. "She likes big things next to small things, but, like, the same things." He looked frustrated trying to explain it.

"Like having a regular nickel next to the giant nickel," Sue said.

Ms. Dira nodded. "Sounds like Sue might be a builder or an artist, or maybe she will design amusement parks and roadside attractions. Do you understand what I am saying to you?"

"That we have things we love to do?" Barry asked.

"Yes. Those things are yours. They are yours whether your parents fight or get along. They are yours no matter what happens. Your parents are choosing to go to war. You can choose to focus on the things you love."

"We love our parents," said Barry. Sue nodded.

"They love you, too. You are their children but you are also your own people. Let them have their war if that's what they choose to do. You did not cause their war and you cannot stop it. When they are done, they will be very proud of the choices you have made, and you will have found a way to create your own happiness. Then you will have something that makes you happy no matter what happens in your life."

"Marbles make you happy?" Sue asked.

"Marbles make me very happy," said Ms. Dira. "Tell you what. Why don't you each choose one of my marbles? Keep it in your pocket, and when you feel like you are being drawn into your parents' war, you can hold your marble and think of the things that are yours that make you happy."

Barry quickly chose a red one. Sue took more time, examining a green one with sparkles before deciding on a marble that had blue and yellow winding through it. They tucked their marbles away in their pockets.

The family center door opened. Their father came in. He looked flustered.

"Let's go, kids," he said. "Your mother has already eaten up fifteen minutes of my time with you."

Sue and Barry waved goodbye to Ms. Dira and left. They got into their father's car.

"What do you love to do?" Sue asked their father.

"We're going to hit traffic," he replied.

Sue felt the marble in her pocket.

Then she reached across the car seat and took hold of her brother's hand.

And held on tight.

11

The Hope Chair

Jafar is not sitting.

He is running.

He is running a happy run. A work-for-the-day-is-done run. A heading-to-school-and-food run, the best run of them all.

Jafar runs on feet made tough from heat and use. Feet that can pound pavement and fly over gravel without hardly noticing the small sharp stones.

Jafar runs through the city, a city that he knows so well he could probably navigate it blindfolded. Every day is the same, yet every day is also different. Sometimes a rain has just ended and the air smells washed of all the engine grime and cook-fire smoke. Sometimes he sees a shopkeeper he hasn't seen in a week and they wave at each other. Sometimes a stray mama dog has a new batch of puppies, and Jafar coaxes them out from beneath the rubbish bin so that he can pet their tiny heads and look into their big, big eyes.

Today, though, there is no stopping for puppies. There is no stopping for anything.

Today there is only running.

He runs through streets that have given him shelter in doorways when a sudden rain starts to fall. He runs under bridges and along a river where his family once had a shack, until the developers bulldozed it away. He runs by the spot where his friend sold batteries until a delivery truck backed up and crushed him.

Each block, each street, each building, each rubbish tip holds pieces of Jafar's life.

He sees himself as a toddler, his mother pouring water over him on the sidewalk in an endless effort to keep him clean. He sees the river where he helps his mother do the laundry, scrubbing the family's clothes on rocks. He sees the recycling depot where he would go with his father, each carrying sacks of trash they would turn into money. The gutter where he found the ball that day, bright green and highly bouncy, small enough to fit into his pocket. The closed gate of the private school where he gave that green ball to a boy who was shaking the gates and crying. The corner where he hawked newspapers when he was eight. The shop where he stole crackers when he couldn't find work and where his mother made him return them. The tiny park where he played with a tiny kitten that was in the arms of a tiny girl.

Jafar is all over this city. Sometimes he waves to the shadows of his former self, but not today. Today he is not interested in remembering. Today is all about looking forward.

Forward is why he is running to school.

Jafar's school is deep in a maze. Outsiders would never find it, but what outsider would even try? A tangle of freeway flyovers gives shelter to a city within a city, beneath the freeway. What started as for-the-moment has now been around since his grandparents were children.

There are many ways into this city. Many narrow alleys that turn and end without warning. It is a city that changes shape daily, when someone new moves in and claims a section of the alley for their own. A wall of tarp and cardboard goes up, and another family has a home.

Jafar's family has a home here, one small room like all the others. Electricity comes sometimes. The lucky families have a fan. Jafar's family doesn't.

"A piece of folded-up paper will give you just as much breeze, and it won't stop working unless you stop working," his mother often says.

On especially hot nights, Jafar falls asleep with her waving a paper over him and his baby brother. It makes him feel like a king.

The lucky, lucky families have a small television set that fetches in kickboxing matches, singing competitions and yacky politicians, all grainy and sometimes green if the color doesn't hold.

Mothers and grandmothers cook in the alleys on small fires placed along the cement walls of the flyover, away from the cardboard walls of their homes.

Children play tag and cat's cradle and other games where the rules are made up as they go along. Men play cards and gossip in groups, smoking hand-rolled cigarettes and drinking homemade booze out of small plastic bags.

Jafar's school is in the middle of the gambling dens and the places girls are taken when they are young and then kicked out two years later when they have turned very, very old.

People know Jafar and he knows them. He knows who will greet him and who will cheat him, who will ignore him and who, if given the chance, will hit him.

He runs through the sights, smells and sounds.

And then he gets to his school.

Where the world is gray, the school is green. A piece of old green artificial grass cleanly covers the floor.

Where the world is noisy and full of dashing, the school is calm. Books sit straight on shelves, chalk sits in tidy rows by the blackboard and foot-wear is put in a line against the wall as soon as children walk through the door.

The teacher, Miss Lily, is always neat as a pin. And she wears a pin! She has a different brooch on every day, pinned to her bright white blouse. She makes the brooches and sells them to earn money for the school.

This is a school for working children. The teacher works, too, in a clothing factory, sewing dresses for ladies in other countries. Her boss lets her bring scraps of cloth to the school. Mothers take them home and make quilts to sell so the school can buy more books and pens.

Jafar runs into the school room. Then he stops running. He has no shoes to take off, but he wipes his feet vigorously on the rough mat at the door. He greets Miss Lily with a bow of his head and a smile. He washes his hands and face in the basin, then loads up a banana leaf with rice, fish and vegetables. He takes his place on the green grass carpet and looks up at his teacher.

"Last week we talked about poetry," she says. "Today we are talking about stories. We humans have been telling each other stories as far back as we can remember. Stories about families, stories about children, stories about work and danger, about love and funny animals. We *are* these stories, and these stories are us."

Jafar wolfs down his meal, clears away his banana leaf and gets his notebook out from his little cubby. He keeps listening while the teacher talks about some of the famous storytellers of history. He sits back down, his pen ready.

"Stories can come from many places," the

teacher says. "They come from every country, from every group of people. From people who are very, very rich and from people who work very hard for everything they get."

"Like us," says one of the students.

"Stories can also be sparked by anything — any day, any moment, any person, any thought, any object. Who can give us some things that might spark a story for you?"

"Taking tickets on a bus," says a boy who had a job doing just that until he got pushed into traffic and hurt his foot. Now he sells chewing gum.

That starts a flood of ideas.

"Bananas," says a child.

"Gold," says another.

"Teachers!" says another child, and everyone laughs.

Jafar's brain is on fire. He knows, knows, knows his idea is good.

He raises his hand and waves it in the air.

"What about chairs?" he asks.

"Everybody sits," the teacher says. "Everybody has sat. Chairs are a good spark for a story. Jafar, can you come up with some story ideas that involve sitting?"

Jafar bends over his notebook, his pen moving faster than he can breathe.

> *With this chair*
> *I am there.*

Jafar sings stories out to the world, and the world, in turn, sings back to him.

Deborah Ellis is the author of more than two dozen books, including *The Breadwinner*, which has been published in twenty-five languages and has recently been released as a film. She has won the Governor General's Award, the Middle East Book Award, the Peter Pan Prize, the Jane Addams Children's Book Award and the Vicky Metcalf Award for a Body of Work. She has received the Ontario Library Association's President's Award for Exceptional Achievement, and she has been named to the Order of Canada. Deb has donated more than $1 million in royalties to organizations such as Women for Women in Afghanistan, UNICEF and Street Kids International. She lives in Simcoe, Ontario.